THE YOGI

Vishal Chaudhary

First published in 2021 by

Becomeshakespeare.com

One Point Six Technologies Pvt Ltd.
119-123, 1st Floor, Building J2, B - Wing,
WadalaTruck Terminal, Wadala East, Mumbai,
Maharashtra, India, 400022.
T:+91 8080226699

ISBN - 978-93-5438-832-3

Contents

Chapter 1

The story begins with an incident at a science lab, where two scientist Charlie and his co-scientist James are discussing about their current project and research on 'Mutation and Water Memory Theory'.

<u>Timing is 10:00 PM</u>

James – 'Hey Charlie', what do you have to say about our brand new invention of 'Mutation through Genes' and giving 'The Fire Powers' to a human through this mutation?

Charlie – James! I am extremely happy about it and I think we are soon going to be very famous for this 'INVENTION' and will be recognized in the scientist's community for this.

James {smirked with fake expressions on his face} – Yes, Of course! The whole world will know our names for this invention.

During the discussion, James phone starts ringing and to attend it he goes to a corner. At that time Charlie goes to his desk and starts working on the last paper that is to be published.

After finishing his work, Charlie stands up and starts calling out James name. He also finds out that James has bolted the lab and has gone somewhere.

After waiting for some time Charlie finds flight ticket receipts to America in the name of James of the same night. Charlie being very shocked starts to call James on his phone but that too is switched off. Charlie goes back to his desk and starts searching all the activities done by James via email. Charlie searches the bank accounts and other files of their research and comes to know that James has transferred all the money from their labs joint account to his private account. He also has deleted all the research files from the desktop as well as the backups. Though, being very depressed Charlie still starts investigating further for some evidence and finds a short video message from James.

"Into the message"

JAMES WITH VERY EVELISH STATE-MENTS-

Charlie! You fool, what did you think that I will leave all this research for a fool like you so that you can give that **"Billion Dollar Formulae"** to the public for free?

How in the hell could you even think you bastard! I am taking all this research with me and will sell it for billions to the right person in my name. I alone will have all the profits, name and fame and you… still will be a poor scientist with no money or fame.

Video Message Ends.

Charlie after listening to this video goes into

an extreme shock, becomes wild with anger and starts destroying the lab with a baseball bat which is present in the lab.

As Charlie is smashing things in the lab lot of noises can be heard. He smashes anything that is in his lab but finds no peace and starts drinking alcohol. As he is very depressed, he attempts to do suicide. Though he is drunk he takes his car keys and starts driving at a very high speed to the beach where he has decided to drown himself in the deep ocean.

On the other hand there is a big party going on a cruise at the sea shore where Charlie has gone to attempt suicide

On the cruise a birthday is being celebrated.

The birthday girl's name is Arvi, whose father is a very wealthy businessman of the area.

Arvi to her Father - "Thanks Papa", for this wonderful party on my 15th Birthday!

Her Father - You are Welcome! My child you know how much your father loves you!

Arvi hugs her father and kisses him, she then thanks him again. On this her father tell her "come my child let's do the cake cutting ceremony".

The cruise is very beautifully decorated for the celebration and every guest can't stop whispering and talking about the wonderful arrangements. Arvi and her father in the meantime are moving slowly towards the table for cutting the cake, suddenly, Boom! A blast takes place on the cruise and some people in the party take out their guns and start firing bullets at everyone. A happy party is immediately turned into a horrible site with all dead bodies around. The goons have been sent by a competitor, a rival in business so that he could finish this competition once and for all. Everyone on the cruise dies and the birthday girl who is nearly half dead starts sinking into the ocean.

Charlie, the scientist is watching all the incidents and the burning cruise from the shore. Now he who has been standing from the last past half an hour is in two minds and has a conflict within himself, whether to do suicide or not.

As the girl Arvi keeps on sinking into the

ocean, she finally hits the bottom of it where other living beings of the water are living in an underground ocean city. There are many water creatures and they have a leader known as the God of the Ocean.

As Arvi goes into a very critical condition near to her death bed, all the water creatures are first very scared of her as they have never seen a human being before but as they soon realize that she about to die they take her to their leader who as mentioned before the "God of the Ocean" and asks him to heal her as it is their duty and responsibility to not allow a human being die in their presence and their city.

However, in the beginning the leader is hesitant

to heal her and says "NO" as he has nothing do with her and nor does he care if she dies or not.

As all the creatures start requesting their leader to not let her die in front of them and after persistent request, finally their leader is convinced and says that he will heal her.

The God of the Ocean then with his powers and old aquatic healing techniques helped the girl Arvi to get better. He also gave her the powers of controlling and bending water by placing a blue shinning pebble on her forehead. As the tides start hitting the shore Arvi in an unconscious state comes to the shore where the scientist Charlie is still in a dilemma of whether to commit suicide or not. He then see a shining stone from a long distance. As the body is not visible in the dark, he starts moving closer to it and finds out that it a girl in a very serious condition with a very low heartbeat. Charlie drops the idea of committing suicide and takes a courageous decision of saving her without knowing who she is and what happened. He takes her to the lab.

The next day Charlie is listening to the news and he finds out that the girls name is Arvi. Each and every news channels are flashing about the incident that took place on the cruise and that her whole family had died in the blast. The news also reported about firing that took place on the cruise.

Now knowing her background Charlie finally decides to raise her as his own daughter.

Arvi is now with Charlie for nearly 5 to 6

months. She starts calling him her father as she has lost all her memory. Charlie while looking after her and treating her finds out that she is not a normal human being but is a "Gifted Child"

While raising Arvi, Charlie goes through many obstacles like he covered her forehead all the time so that nobody could see the blue shining stone, Arvi would also get panic attacks of the incident that took place on the cruise where her parents were killed, she would get into arguments and fights at school and what not.

Hence, Charlie after giving up all hopes on her to improve, he took it on himself to teach her on his own and also train her to control the powers and emotions to use them in a positive manner.

By now Arvi grew up into a very beautiful woman with having full control and accumulation of her power. The build-up power within her could create a lot of disaster that easily could happen as all those raising years of her, Charlie the scientist was working on water memory theory so that he could bring back Arvi's memory and actually it works. Arvi gets back her memory that she had lost during the cruise incident and decides to take revenge from the goons who had killed her parents.

Arvi to Charlie – Father! Shall I take revenge from those bastards who killed my parents?

Charlie – It is completely your decision. You have to decide yourself whether to do it or not. I can feel your emotions as losing parents at a young age is very hard face of life.

While saying this Charlie switches on the television and the first news that he hears is that his co-scientist James, who had stolen all his research had been doing mutation experiments on his secretary by giving her the "Power of Fire". James named her 'Jwala' (the fire lady). However, after being mutated the first thing that she does, kills James as he has been physically exploiting her for a very long time

DURING THIS MOMENT:

Jwala to James – You bastard, this is your last day to be alive, get ready to die.

James- Please! Jwala, "don't kill me", I beg you, I am your boss and also the main reason behind getting you these powers.

Jwala – No! You rascal, "You don't deserve to stay alive", as I know how much you have exploited me.

She shoots fire flames at him by which James immediately dies and turns into ashes.

After killing James, Jwala becomes very destructive and hence is all over the news for her bad sins and the murder of James the scientist who is her boss.

Charlie and Arvi decide to stop her. Charlie by that time is not aware but still senses that Jwala is the by-product of this own research work.

In order to stop Jwala from doing any more destruction Charlie and Arvi (the Aqua Girl) goes to the lab where James was experimenting on Jwala for the fire mutation. As soon as they reach the lab they find a very big broken photo frame of his co-scientist and Charlie is now 100% convinced that Jwala is a result of his experimental formulae and research.

While Charlie is at the lab, Arvi has reached the area where Jwala is destroying the whole city. There is a crisis that arises whether to kill Jwala or not. All this incidents as being shown on the television. Charlie sees this and gets into his car and reaches the site where already a massive fight is going on between the two superwomen's.

The fight between Fire and Water – As both superwomen are indulged in their fight, all around there are flames of fire and jets of water that is controlling the fire that Jwala is spreading.

Charlie – The scientist Charlie reaches the place of the fight and screams loudly in order to stop their fight by stating that they are related as sisters in some way.

However, both of them do not listen to him and Jwala also attacks Charlie making him unconscious. Seeing Charlie in this condition Arvi becomes extremely angry and outrageous that finally changes into a massive showdown fight between the two ladies. Finally, Arvi wins the fight against Jwala. Using her full power

Arvi is able to know Jwala unconscious while doing so Arvi too gets injured. Charlie regains consciousness and takes both the ladies to the lab to save their lives.

At this moment Charlie the scientist has been able to find two superhuman and is yet to find five more. The third super hero is named 'Patther' (stone) which now they have to find.

Chapter 2

The next chapter story is about a very decent and simpler person by the name 'Randheer' who is dedicated to his job and is a very hard working employee of a chemical based company. A provoking incident happens as Randheer is a very curious employee steps into the restricted zone of the company where a highly secretive chemical is being made that can increase bone density and make them lighter as well. This chemical can decrease the body mass of a person that results into strong and light body that reduces the effect of gravity on that particular person.

Randheer is suddenly caught for being in the restricted area.

Guards – Who are you? And what are you doing here?

Randheer- I am an employee of this company and I came here searching for someone.

Saying this he somehow manages to come out from the restricted area and takes a pleasant breath. However, all this incident now arises more curiosity in Randheer about the area and the project that is going on. He attempts to get into the place on a daily bases. One fine day he does get a chance to enter the area after office hours and when there are very few employees around.

He starts searching the area after some time he comes to know that the CEO of the company is making a formulae to sell it to a terrorist group so that they can make their own army of super strong people. Randheer being curious, nervous and tensed still steals a sample of the formulae to test it in his lab. After returning to his lab that is in his house he privately tests the formulae on himself. As he lives alone in the house, he first tests it on a rat and finds no reaction and continues to test it on himself that creates a chemical reaction in his body making him very light in body but too hard on his upper layer skin that is like a stone.

On the other hand Arvi and Charlie are trying to re-fix the mutation genes of Jwala so that she could be recovered from her unconscious state that had occurred due to the fight between her and Arvi.

Charlie from one of his source find about Randheer who was working in a chemical factory has gone through a mutation and has not been coming to office since the day he had the accident. In order to find him, Arvi and Charlie go to his apartment but come to know from his neighbours that he has locked himself there since last week has not come out at all.

Both, Arvi and Charlie start knocking on his door (Voice is heard within the apartment) Who the fuck is this?

Charlie – You don't know us, but we know all about you and your accident that took place at the lab.

Randheer from Inside – You fools! You don't know anything. Just go away from here if you really care for your lives and don't want to die.

As he says this Arvi uses her power and hits the door with a high pressure water jet and both of them get inside the apartment. At that moment Randheer tries to hit them in self-defence but Arvi stops him and ask him to go and sit on the sofa as all they needed was to talk to him about the consequences that he is facing after the accident.

Then all of them start discussing and talking, Randheer tells them the whole incident and the way he started looking after that totally ugly. After talking to him Arvi and Charlie return to the lab.

In the meantime Randheer wants revenge from the company for what he turned into. He decides to kill the CEO of the company as well as all the people involved in making the dangerous formulae. The CEO of the company comes to know that one of the sample has been stolen from the lab but does not pay attention to it seriously as he has whole army of mutated beings and no one can touch or kill him.

As the CEO is talking to other employees and people involved in the experiment the decorum of the place gets disturbed and the guards find out that someone has entered the premises and is trying to kill people. The CEO of the company then gives orders to kill whoever he is.

An army of 20 mutated soldiers start to descend to the ground to full fill their bosses' orders. There is fight between an only mutated person Radheer and all the mutated army. Due to the fight there are lot of dead bodies and blood all around but still the fight continues. The CEO seeing all this comes on the battleground, he has taken the formulae and hence is mutated. Radheer keeps on fighting with the rest of the army but is nearly defeated.

Radheer is beaten up so badly by the army that he almost dies, all of them think that he is dead and they pick him up and dumps his body in a massive container with radioactive dump of the company. Arvi and Charlie have already visited the company a day before and hence ask the guard to tell them if anything wrong has taken place. After the incident the guard immediately calls them and tells them about the incident that happened in the company and also mentions that the army dumped Radheer body into the radioactive garbage.

Without wasting time Arvi and Charlie start their car and hurry up to reach to the incident place. There they find an unconscious Radheer in the dump, they immediately take his body to the lab and after doing few experiments on his body they come to know that he has become stronger than before. During all this experiment Radheer is unconscious but suddenly wakes up and starts to shout.

"I will kill those bastards! Who ruined my whole life, "I will kill all of them.... AAAAAAAAAAA

Arvi and Charlie give him some anaesthesia so that he does not create any more destruction. When the effect of the anaesthesia reduces Radheer regains conscious. In the lab he sees Arvi, Jwala, Charlie and his assistant. Randheer tries to convince them to help him by telling them about the plans of the CEO of the company. The CEO wants to build an army of mutated beings to rule the whole world and them. Listening to all this Jwala who is furious speaks up.

Jwala – We will not allow him to do such a thing and I will fight till my last breadth to defend the Human race.

Arvi- Yes we will and won't allow anybody to do such kind of selfish destruction. We all are in this fight together.

Hearing their opinion and willing to help, Randheer was all pumped up with excitement and positive feelings as he had nobody's help to win this battle alone. After a big discussion Arvi and Jwala showed their powers to Radheer who had no reaction on his face. Charlie who was watching this from a corner started to smile and told all of them not to show off their powers as it was not an exhibition.

Suddenly, a news flashed on the television that an army of mutants attacked the parliament and other historical monuments. They were destroying anything and everything that came in their way.

Radheer (In his loud voice) – Girls! It's time to get ready, we have to go for a mission

All of them suit up and take off to the place where the mutants are creating havoc and destroying things.

At the place of destruction the villain holds a mike and speaks that anyone who would come in his or his army's path would be immediately executed and killed.

At that moment all of our 3 Super Heroes reach the place of action and start fighting with help of their respective powers. Arvi with a heavy and pressurised water spray attacks the mutated villain and the whole army get furious and attacks all three of them. As the scientist Charlie has no power keeps watching all this behind a big stone and gives his little inputs time to time like throwing some gradates and continuously firing at the army with the gun.

The fight continues making the atmosphere tensed as to who is going to win the fight. As we all know that Good always wins over the bad and our superheroes win the fight killing all the mutants and their leader. The police squad reaches the site of action but by that time all the superheroes have vanished trying to reach their lab as soon as possible.

To return to their lab Arvi jumps into the water, Jwala flies away and the other two start their car and drive on full speed so that they can reach their lab without being caught.

Chapter 3

As all of them reach the lab they find a young, smart man already sitting in the lab waiting for them to come. All of them think that he is their enemy and hence Patthar(Randheer) attacks him but as the person is the master of Air he without using his hand dodges the attacks and explains "I am not here to fight, I am just here for asking help". My predecessor has been murdered by one of his own student who now has become very powerful and has taken over the place where they practise and live.

Jwala suddenly asks the person "What is your name and where the place where you live?"

Arvi – "Why the hell has that student killed your master? And sorry what was his name again?

Master of Air(Pavan) – " I am the last master of Air besides 'Brut', the one who killed our master in order to full fill his greed of getting the masters position and powers. The person then beings to tell them about what actually happened. He mentions that their school of Martial Arts is located in a very secret area and only people belonging to that place can only enter.

He then starts to narrate the actual incident, one fine day as he was out of the campus to fetch fresh water' Brut' killed the master in his absence and when he returned he found the whole place destroyed and some junior students dead in the campus. Once Brut killed the master he announced a bounty on Pavan's head that is whoever would kill him would get a handsome amount of money. After Pavan came to know about this deal he decided to go underground for many days as it was not possible for him to fight alone. While doing so he got injured and tried to save his life. His master had given him a letter in which the lab address had been written and that they were the only one that could save and help him in this case. Since then he is roaming around to find the other Masters of the Chakras.

He also further states that there are two people of his community who have left but out of which one has very devilish thoughts of ruling the whole world and he will kill anyone who comes in his way.

After listening to Pavan, the superhero tell him that we do not believe you or in the techniques existences.

Randheer – I also do not believe in this shit

Pavan then smiles and says to all of them "Look at yourself! You are far different from the normal human being and still you people are not willing to believe in me.

The scientist, Charlie is listening to all this conversation silently and knows that Pavan is speaking the truth.

Charlie speaks up and says that he himself has been to that place and Pavan's father was his friend!

Charlie further says that you are not the only 4 Masters but there are three more who have their own power of energy, time and space respectively and this is just the beginning as many fights have to be fought and hence should help Pavan in order to maintain peace.

The three superheroes except for Pavan get very surprised about Charlies knowledge and keeping it to himself and not telling them. Hence, they leave the lab in an anger saying that they are not into this and are not going to help them.

However, the following next day they find out through the television news that Pavan was telling the truth and the villain 'Brut' was becoming more stronger and destructive like a monster.

They come to know that he has murdered a lot of people to full fill his selfish intensions of ruling the world. After listening to the news they all decide to help Pavan for the sake of good and return to the lab.

Charlie – Why have you three come back? You were not going to help us in this….

Arvi- We have listened to the new and now that you both cant alone defeat Brut hence we are here to help.

Jwala- Yes, Charlie you can't do this all alone!

Patthar (Randheer) – Yes! You can't

After listening to all their conversations Charlie ask them to get suit up for the fight that could take place any time.

All of the super heroes get dressed up and practise; showing off their skills and powers to each other.

Arvi displayed her power and skills by throwing water from her hands.

Jwala displayed her power and skills by shooting flames.

Pavan too displayed his power and skills of bending air by not letting the fire spread by making a massive face and stopping all the fire at once.

Finally doing all these small entrainments they

leave the lab to reach the place of destruction and fight to stop Brut.

However, before leaving the lab they had some plans about the fight and discussion on who will do what. They also distribute all their work separately.

Finally, the fight between the Masters and Villain begins. Fire and water are spread all around the pace, Pavan is helping Jwala with bending air to increase the potential of the fire shoots by Jwala.

Patthar (Randheer) is hitting and smashing every one as he is very strong like a mountain and is not impacted by any fire flames or water jets.

They use their potential to the fullest and

defeat all the goons and villain and now only 'Brut' is left but is a critical condition due to the injuries. He is very powerful and fights till his last breadth by bending all the flame of fire reaching to him. However, in the end he is defeated.

But it is the best bender 'Pavan' who fights with him. He kills and defeats him in order to maintain peace and take his masters revenge.

Chapter 4

The chapter begins with the introduction of a new character named 'Urjit', who real name is 'Koranga'. He is a mechanical engineer and has been working along with his colleague 'Abhram' on a project of never ending power source which works on the principle of multiple fusion and generates a great amount of electrical energy.

Urjit – Hey Abhram! It's almost done now. We

just have to do few experiments in order to find out that it is working perfectly or not.

Abhram- Ya! Sure, I am completely with you and will be always with you at every situation.

Urjit- Thanks a lot buddy. There is no one in my life except you…. Who has been always with me?

They both go to different private companies to sell their invention. They also went to the companies who ridiculed their vision on invention.

One of the company steal their idea and sends them back by saying that they are not interested. After few days both of them find out via news that the company who asked them to leave, is selling their same invention to some other big company without giving any credit and royalty.

Seeing this Urjit becomes very angry

Urjit- Abhram!!! I will destroy these mother fuckers for stealing my life time research idea and invention.

Abhram- I am always with you. Do whatever you wish to do with these bastards.

On the other hand all the Masters are asking Charlie about his truth and previous life and how he already knows what is going to happen, as previously he revealed some of his secrets that he is trying to bring all the 7 Chakras Masters together in order to get enlightened as by doing so he will be able to open all of his 7 Chakras.

Charlie (Reveals the Truth)

He tells them that he is Yogi whose age is even more than the total sum of all their ages and this fight is between the Good and the Bad.

Due to this fight it has become very crucial of brining all the 7 Chakra Masters together. Listening to Charlie all the Masters become aware that they are all together and all of this is predestined to find out the purpose of their life.

As they are discussing this 'Urjit' is all over the news for destroying the company who stole his invention along with the help of his friend Abhram.

Urjit starts becoming powerful day by day that he cannot be defeated alone as he is very fast and has a latest upgraded suit which can go through very high voltage electric shock waves, other small weapons and gadgets.

Hence, a crisis arise between the other Masters whether to kill him or not.

During the discussion between the Masters

Arvi- We should kill him as he has already created lot of destruction and is no use to us.

Pavan- Ya! We should

Jwala and Patthar also present their views and take a call that Urjit should be killed.

On this Charlie says

Charlie- We cannot kill him as he is the only Master of energy. Rather we can destroy his energy source and gadgets to make him our prisoner.

The other Masters also support the idea and are convinced to do so. But by now Urjit has already destroyed all the 5 companies who insulted him and made fun of his invention. He kills lot of people including the CEO's….

The news is flashing all over, so they search for the location where all this is taking place to stop Urjit from damaging more. As they reach there they ask Urjit to stop but refuses to do so and keeps on killing people.

On this Arvi throws a water splash on him in order to save him from this attack Urjit creates a high voltage current pass through which directly hits Arvi. Then both Jwala and Pavan tries the power of fire and air but still do not get a result.

The Masters finally come together and strategically kill Urjit's friend Abhram. Seeing this Urjit gets very depressed and the Masters make him loose his power source without which he is now just an ordinary person.

They make him a prisoner and put him in a van so that they can take him to the lab.

Urjit shouts- I will sue you all and will make you beg for what you all have done.

Charlie- Will you please keep your mouth shut for a while till we reach the lab. This is all done for your safety and protection so stop yelling at us.

Urjit does not listen and continues to shout and abuse each one of them who are present in the van.

Patthar (Randheer) punches him hard and stops the shouting and yelling. They finally take him to the lab along with other Masters.

Chapter 5

The chapter starts with a young couple of Indian origin studying in a university of Japan and working on duality of matter that is Quantum Physics.

As both of them are working with each other for a very long they fall in love and they invent a device that can help to travel through time but also travel through space as duality of matter or the Butterfly effect is the main criteria defining everything happening all around a person , object or world.

On the other hand all the 5 Masters are together for the sake of peace. As the couple start becoming successful in creating the device to travel through time both of them start to have fun. As we already know that travelling through space is to travel through time and vice versa. With the help of the device they travel to any place at any time.

The female discovers that as they travel through space and time, both of those also travel with them resulting in the diminishing of their love as distance arises between them due to difference of opinions.

Jenny to Samay- I am not finding this

interesting anymore as it is affecting us and our relationship.

Samay- I don't care about anything! I am enjoying the invention that I have created.

Jenny- Ok then I am leaving as I can't support you any more

Samay- Ok so go away and need not come back

Samay the last Master seems to enjoy all that is happening unware of what is going to happen but Jenny on the other hand is aware that the life that is deriving through themselves is getting altered due to this time travelling and time lap jumps.

However, by that time Samay has become

crazy after losing his love and is trying to drive time according to him by setting the device to transport him to many places at the same time which leads to the increase in the time to enlightenment.

As all the masters are aware of this, they ask Jenny for help.

As she is aware of what is happening Jenny agrees to help them.

All the Masters are unaware of the whereabouts of the last Master that is the Master of Time. So with the help of Jenny they make a plan to catch him and convince him that he is the only Master of Time among all the rest of the Masters and whatever he is doing is not good for the human race.

Instead of listening to them he gets more angry and outrageous as he is thinking that his love as betrayed him by helping the other Masters to catch him.

A fight takes place between 'Samay' and the other Masters.

As he is the Master of Time, he makes a copy of himself from a different time zone and defeats the other Masters single handily.

However, at the end Charlies convincing power and the love of Samay for Jenny, he asks Samay to help them and begs him for the life of the other Masters and the human race.

As Samay is a true lover, he agrees for the same and also comes to know that all of them were speaking the truth. Hence, he stops fighting and joins as one of the Seven Masers. At this stage of the saga all the Masters have been brought together.

Chapter 6

All the Seven Masters are together and hence they can all be seen in one single frame, talking with each other about themselves and their powers. Charlie is sitting in a corner as if he not there with closed eyes and listening to each one of them, he realizes that it has been a very long time since they have been talking and ask them to be quiet as their voices are striking his head and pinching his ears.

Charlie: Hey you all! Please be quiet as your voices are sticking into my head.

There is no response from anyone

Charlie again speaks out will you all be quiet or not? He suddenly hears a voice.

Hey who are you talking to? This voice was of another person sitting next to Charlie while doing meditation along with him. Charlie then opens his eyes and finds no one near him but he can only see one person in the same room sitting who has been meditating since last 6 months at the very same place.

Suddenly, the other person sitting next to Charlie saw a light of enlightenment coming within himself as well as Charlie. As both of them were enlightened and found full control over all their seven chakras that are Muladhar Chakra, Swadistan Chakra, Nabhi Chakra, Anhat Chakra, Visudhit Chakra, Aagya Chakra and Sasthar Chakra.

Both of the individuals are smiling as if they have received some treasure and a light can be seen all around. The truth is that all the seven super heroes were actually the 7 Chakras; each of the super heroes represented each of the Chakras.

The main goal of both persons was to sit and mediate to get full control over each and every 'Chakra' within their body